For Gina
—J. D.

With all my love for my daughters, Sophie and Katie Rose
—D. G.

Library of Congress Cataloging-in-Publication Data
Dunbar, Joyce.
Tell me something happy before I go to sleep/Joyce Dunbar;
[illustrated by] Debi Gliori. —1st U.S. ed.
p. cm.
Summary: Willa has trouble falling asleep until her brother reminds her of
all the happy things that await her in the morning.
ISBN 0-15-201795-X
[1. Rabbits—Fiction. 2. Bedtime—Fiction. 3. Brothers and sisters—Fiction.]
I. Gliori, Debi, ill. II. Title.
PZ7.D8944Td 1998
[E]—dc21 97-38562

First U.S. edition 1998
First published in Great Britain in 1998 by Doubleday,
a division of Transworld Publishers Ltd.
C E G H F D

Printed in Mexico

Tell Me Something Happy Before I Go to Sleep

JOYCE DUNBAR • DEBI GLIORI

Harcourt Brace & Company

San Diego   New York   London

Willa was tired,
so Willa went to bed.

She lay with her pillow this way . . .
and that way . . . and another way.
But Willa couldn't sleep.

"Willoughby," called Willa. "Are you there?"

"Yes," answered Willoughby. "I'm here."

"I can't sleep," said Willa.

"Why can't you sleep?" asked Willoughby.

"I'm afraid," said Willa.

"What are you afraid of?" asked Willoughby.

"I'm afraid that I might have a bad dream," said Willa.

"Think of something happy, then you won't have a bad dream," said Willoughby.

So Willa tried to think of something happy, but she couldn't.

"Willoughby," called Willa. "Are you still there?"

"Yes," answered Willoughby. "I'm still here."
"What can I think of that's happy?" asked Willa.
"Oh, lots of things," said Willoughby.
"Tell me. Tell me something happy before I go to sleep."

Willoughby thought for a moment. Then he said, "Willa, look under your bed."

So Willa leaned over and looked under her bed.
"What do you see?" asked Willoughby.
"I see my chicken slippers," said Willa.
"That's right," said Willoughby.

"And do you know what your chicken slippers are doing?"

"No," said Willa. "I don't."

"They are waiting, just waiting, for nobody's feet but yours."

"Good," said Willa. "That's happy. What else?"

"What do you see on the chair?" asked Willoughby.

"I see my blue-and-white jumpsuit," said Willa.

"Do you know what your jumpsuit is doing?" asked Willoughby.

"No," said Willa. "I don't."

"It is longing, just longing, for tomorrow, when you will jump out of bed and put it on."

"Good," said Willa. "That's happy. What else?"

Willoughby picked Willa up in his arms and padded softly downstairs to the kitchen. He opened the pantry door.

"What do you see on the shelves?" asked Willoughby.

"I see bread and honey and oats and milk and apples," said Willa.

"That's right," said Willoughby, "all waiting to be made into breakfast, for you and me to share."

"Oh good," said Willa. "That's happy. What else?"

Willoughby carried Willa into the living room and switched on the lamp.

"What do you see in the corner?" asked Willoughby.

"I see my basket full of toys," said Willa.

"What do you think they are doing?" asked Willoughby.

"I don't know," said Willa.

"They are dreaming, dreaming of tomorrow, and the games you are going to play."

"That's very happy," said Willa. "What else?"

Willoughby carried Willa to the window and opened the curtains wide.

"What do you see in the darkness?" asked Willoughby.

"I see only the night," said Willa.

"What do you think the night is doing?" asked Willoughby.

"I don't know," said Willa.

"The night is waiting, waiting for the morning, which is on its way round the world."

"That's happy," said Willa.

"The morning is waiting, too," said Willoughby.

"What for?" asked Willa.

"Oh, lots of things," said Willoughby.

"What things?" asked Willa.

"For grass to grow, flowers to bloom, and leaves to flutter. For clouds to float, wind to blow, and sun to shine. For birds to fly, bees to buzz, and ducks to quack."

"That's a lot of happy things," said Willa.

"There's just one sad thing," said Willoughby.

"What's that?" asked Willa.

"The morning is waiting for you, too. It's waiting to wake you up."

"But I'm awake already," said Willa.

"That's why it's sad," said Willoughby. "The morning likes waking you up. That's what makes the morning happy."

"Willoughby," said Willa.

"What is it?" asked Willoughby.

"I'm tired."

So Willoughby carried Willa back to bed.

"What do you see in your bed?" asked Willoughby.

"I see my bear," said Willa.

"What do you think he is doing?" asked Willoughby.

"Waiting for me to snuggle up with him," said Willa.

"That's right," said Willoughby, "waiting especially for you."

"And when the morning comes and wakes me up, will you still be here?" asked Willa.

"I'll still be here," said Willoughby.

"Good," said Willa. "That's the happiest thing of all!"

"Good night, Willa."

But Willa didn't answer.
She was sound asleep.

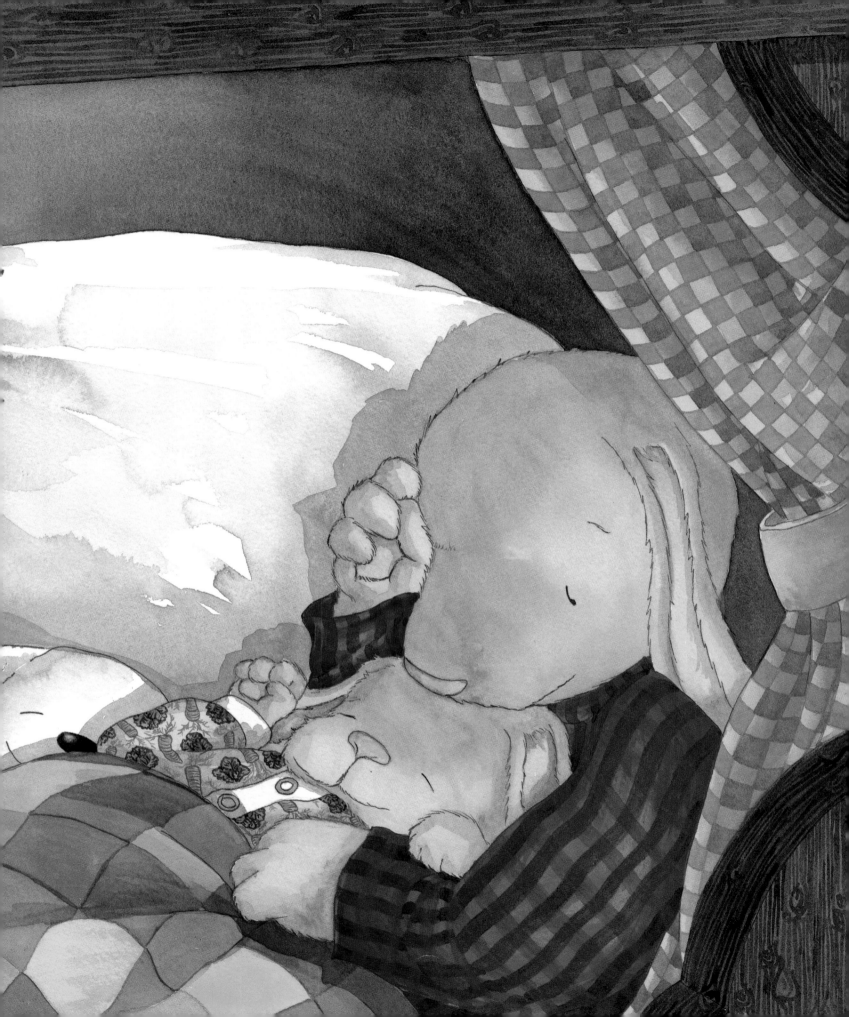